The Golden Fur

LILLIAN COLETTE HUGHES

ISBN: 1981157476
ISBN-13: 978-1981157471

DEDICATION

I would like to dedicate this book to my editor, Christi Hughes; my graphic designer, Clint Hughes; and my little calico kitten, Panchey, who gave me inspiration to start and finish this book, even after her death. To all of you, thank you for everything!

CONTENTS

THE STORY

I watched as the leaves danced across the sky in pretty patterns of color. My mom, my siblings, and I were trotting down a path of twigs. For a cat, the forest is a vast place with many kinds of trees, animals, and plants. It was currently late fall, so we walked quickly to escape the cold breezes.

My name is Autumn, and I am a cat who lives in the woods. I've lived here all my life, and even though I am only seven months old, I know a lot about the part of the forest my family lives in. There are big pine trees and small creeks and yummy prey like rodents to eat. As the sticks crunched under my paws, I trotted along with my family toward our home by the creek. My mom, Summer, mewed to let us know we had arrived. My siblings came behind me with joyful meows and purrs.

My brother, Tango, and my sister, Luna, were wrestling with each other when Mom called "Dinner time!" I was famished, so I left the creek side along with my siblings and sat down beside my mom. She dragged a mole out from beneath a pile of leaves, and let us feast on the delicious dinner. After our meal, Mom started to tell us a story.

"Long ago," began Mom, "there were three star cats named Cloud, Wind, and Rain. One day while they were playing, they got lost. They had been told not to go to the ground, but being carried away by the emotions of curiosity and carefree joy in a game of *Catch the Leaves*, they went anyway. They were all right until wolves started to come after them. They had to make it home to the sky in time, so they did what their mother had always told them to do. They followed the Golden Fur. They followed it away from the wolves and into the sky. And that is how we know that if we are ever lost, we can follow the Golden Fur, which is always high in the sky in the day. Remember, it is that yellow, furry ball in the air. If it is night, then you can follow the three star cats, and they will guide you home."

"Cool!" exclaimed Tango.

"Tell us another one," pleaded Luna.

"Not tonight, but maybe tomorrow. For now I must rest," replied Mom. Upon hearing this, we walked over to her and laid down by her paws, and soon we were all fast asleep.

LOST

As light made its way between the pine trees, I lifted my head and yawned. Luna and Tango were already awake. Mom was swishing her tail through the leaves in search of breakfast. As I got up to stretch my legs, I realized that the creek was very low. "Mom!" I shouted, "What happened to all the water?"

She came over to me and looked down into the creek. A worried expression came over her face. "We have to leave," she announced.

"But why?" asked Tango, who had walked over along with Luna.

"The water will soon be gone," she replied. "It seems the water is drying up, and this is the only river that is in easy access, for the others are either too far away, have too fast of currents, or are too deep. We need water, so we must move on."

We walked through the woods for a while until Mom said we needed to take a break. My stomach growled and I realized I hadn't had breakfast, so I sat down. Luna came up to Mom and said she wanted to play tag.

"Ok," answered Mom, "but don't go too far."

As Luna chased us through the grass, I thought about Mom. "Lets get back," I said, "Mom might be worried."

I was waiting for someone to move when Tango said something that made me shiver. "Um, where exactly is back?"

I watched the butterflies dance in the sky as we hopefully waited for Mom to come and find us, and then we started to walk. It was like an unspoken decision between us. First, Tango got up and started moving, then I followed, and finally Luna joined in. We walked far, over hills and across logs, and we all did it without saying a word. It started to get late, so we stopped at a tree with a hole in the bottom. Luna was pacing back and forth in front of the tree. I could tell she missed Mom a lot.

"Luna," I said, "I know you're upset about losing Mom, but we'll find her, ok?"

She stopped pacing and looked at me. "Ok," she meowed dejectedly, and then she went into the tree with Tango.

I stared at the beautiful night sky trying to find Cloud, Wind, or Rain among the stars. I had no luck, though. I didn't find one star cat much less three.

I turned at the sound of leaves rustling, and a squirrel caught my attention. I crouched low to the ground. I knew that we needed this squirrel because we hadn't eaten all day. I started creeping through the grass. I was about to pounce when I saw its jet-black eyes look up at me. For a second we just stood there, our eyes locked on each other. Then, as if on cue, the squirrel started to run, and I chased after it. I tore through the forest at blinding speed. I reached out my claws expecting to feel just air but, to my relief, I felt fur under my paw as the squirrel was knocked to one side. I bit it and felt it go limp between my jaws. Then, I grasped it firmly in my mouth, and started to walk to the tree.

When Luna and Tango saw the squirrel, they almost tackled me with joy. We gulped the squirrel down in a matter of minutes, and soon enough it was just bones. We were still hungry, but we weren't unsatisfied either. We curled up in a big heap of fur. This helped us stay warm in our little hole in the tree. It wasn't freezing outside, but chilly fall winds blew all around the woods making little critters take shelter. I wanted a story from Mom. I wanted to snuggle with Mom. I wanted to be with Mom, but I couldn't. At least not right now. So, I wiggled my way closer to my siblings and closed my eyes.

DANGER IN THE RIVER

That night, I dreamed about her. She was sprinting through the pine needles, and when she was close enough to hear I heard her say, "Come find me! I am waiting for you!" I was about to answer her and tell her that we were trying when a series of bright lights repeatedly flashed in my eyes.

I woke up and looked out of the tree. There in front of me stood a big group of glowing bugs. I remembered that Mom had told me that they were called fireflies. "Cool!" I thought. I poked Luna and Tango with my paw.

"What?" Tango moaned, "I was trying to slee- whoa! Fireflies!" Luna didn't seem as excited as Tango, but she still thought they were nice.

"Let's follow them!" I suggested, "Maybe they will lead us to Mom!"

"Great idea!" said Luna.

We ventured out into the darkness hoping they would take us to our lost mother. They didn't. Instead, they led us to a river with a racing current and small grey fish. By now, light was poking through the trees and, though the fireflies were harder to see, we could start to make out the things around us in the golden light. Suddenly, I remembered something important.

"I had a dream of Mom last night," I told my siblings, "She said to come find her, and then I woke up. Maybe these fireflies are connected to the dream, and Mom will be somewhere on the other side of this river! Think about it. All we need to do is cross."

"How are we ever going to cross this?" cried Luna.

Tango looked thoughtful, and then spoke up. "I'll start searching the river for a way across. In the meantime, both of you can stay here and rest."

Tango began walking to the left along the river. After about five minutes, we saw him again. This time he walked to the right. We knew he had found something when we heard his loud "*Meow!*" of excitement. We ran over to where he was, and it turned out he had found a vine leading across the river. We were all celebrating happily that we could finally cross the river, but then I took a closer look at the vine. It was long but thin, and covered in slippery, wet moss.

"Are you sure it is safe to cross that, Tango?" I asked.

"Not really, but it's the only way," he responded.

I glanced right to left, and realized that he was correct. I was about to volunteer to go first when Luna spoke up.

"Why can't we just swim across? I hate water, and I know you guys do too, but it sounds a lot easier then crossing on that old vine," she said.

I thought about this, but then Tango made me reconsider. "I like your idea, but the current is too strong. We will get swept away if we swim."

We agreed to cross on the vine. Tango suggested that we go first, so we did. First, Luna went tiptoeing across the vine. She reached the end of it and gave herself a silent cheer. Then she looked our way. I knew it was my turn now, so I started across the vine. At one point I slipped, but I caught myself just in time. When I hopped onto solid ground I felt relieved that the vine walk was over for me. Now it was Tango's turn. He carefully stepped onto the vine, and slowly walked across. He was almost there when some of the slippery moss caught him off guard. He plunged into the river with a deafening yowl, and started to get carried away by the current.

"Tango! Tango!" Luna and I shouted. My heart beat fast as I watched my brother get swept away by the current, and that's when I felt a sudden burst of energy and started to gallop along the riverside.

"Help me!" Tango pleaded. He was about to say something else, but a wave swept over him and he went under.

I ran faster. I gained speed with every leap, until finally I reached where he was. I put my paw into the water, and then tore it out. I hated the way it felt. Still, I had to save Tango, so I dove into the icy cold water and gripped his scruff in my teeth. I tried to haul him out, but the current was throwing me around and I couldn't get my paws back onto dry land! I knew that I might never escape this river and, worst of all, not save Tango, but I did know that the most I could do right then was try. I wouldn't let go of him no matter what happened!

Just as I felt like my lungs were going to burst, I felt Tango's weight getting lighter, and I was able to pull him up on shore. As soon as he was on dry land, I collapsed and started to cough the water out of my aching lungs. We were shivering, cold, and half-drowned, but we were alive.

Luna came over to me. "Thank you for helping me save Tango," I wheezed.

"Any time, Sis." She said this with a warm smile, and it made me feel warmer and happy.

When we were finally able to stand up again, Tango and I limped down to a patch of soft leaves with Luna close behind. I laid down on the soft soil and started to lick myself dry. I thought about the event that had just occurred. I wondered how I suddenly got the energy to go after him, or the determination to not let go. All I knew was that Tango was alive, and that was enough for me.

The next day, I woke up and laid there for a while, just thinking of Mom. I tried to remember her stories to comfort me, but it seemed like I had forgotten all of them. Finally, I got up and woke my siblings. They agreed that we should keep searching, so we abandoned the comfy pile of leaves and started hiking around the colorful forest. As we pressed on, it began to get colder and colder. It was then that I realized that fall was coming to an end, and winter was approaching.

FIRE AND FLAMES

"Autumn," Luna whispered, "when are we going to find Mom?"

"I don't know," I replied, "I hope it's soon."

I decided that I would go hunting. I wanted to do something that took my mind off Mom, and it would give us something to eat. I told my siblings where I was going, and they nodded. I went off into the woods. At first I didn't see anything, but then my luck changed. As I was rummaging through the forest, I spotted a rabbit munching on some berries from a vine. I stalked it for about five minutes, making sure it didn't see me. I was lucky, for this rabbit seemed so focused on the berries that it didn't move or check its surroundings. I took one last look at the rabbit to make sure it was still distracted, and then I pounced. It was an easy kill. I brought it back to my siblings and we ate happily. When we finished the rabbit, I decided we should have a little fun.

"Hey guys, let's chase some leaves and have some fun for a change!" I suggested. We agreed to do that, so we all started pouncing. Sadly, only about five minutes after we started playing, I felt raindrops on my head. Suddenly, a loud clap of thunder rang out through the stormy sky. ***Boom!***

"Ahhhhhhhhh!" We all yowled in unison, and then rushed to a hole in a nearby unfamiliar tree.

Flash! Bolts of lightning lit up the sky as we watched with a mixture of fear and awe. The storm seemed like it would go on forever. We ended up staying in that small hole until the rain started to pound against the small tunnel in waves and the sky turned inky black.

I was staring up at the sky when I saw a lightning bolt streak across the sky…. and hit a tree that was very close to us. Sparks flew everywhere, and I saw a small flame sitting atop the wood. It didn't stay small for long, though. Soon, the whole tree was engulfed in flames!

"Tango, Luna, there's a forest fire starting! We need to leave!" My voice shook in terror as my sibling's expressions turned grim. I nodded my head, and they rose to their paws. Then, we ran. We ran hard as rain pelted our coats and the wind rushed through the trees. We were terrified, and running with no knowledge of where we were going, when Tango shouted something over the howling wind.

"I found a tunnel that seems safe enough! Follow me, and hurry!"

We were sprinting behind Tango and almost to the tunnel

when there was a **crack!** and a flaming tree started to lean over. It was falling right in the direction of Luna! I tried to cry out to warn her, but my voice was lost in the howl of the wind. "Luna!"

She ran on, unaware of the falling tree. She stopped when she heard the creaking noise and looked up. Then there was a loud **crash!** and everything seemed to become soundless. The tree lay there with flames dancing and twisting. I ran over to the log and, with the help of Tango, we tried to roll it over. Our paws felt the hot wood of the tree, and I knew Tango was feeling the searing heat like I was, but I knew Luna had to have felt worse, so I kept pushing. Finally, we were able to slightly move the tree, but what I saw next hurt more than my burnt paws. Luna wasn't there.

I sat on that spot, feeling sadder than ever. Then I heard a soft *"Meow."* I jumped over the log and, on the other side, I found my beloved sister, Luna. "You're alright!" I exclaimed.

"Thankfully," she mewed. Luna explained what had happened. By some miracle, when the tree fell she was able to roll to the side before it hit. I was so relieved I licked her right on the nose. Luna, too tired and surprised to speak, giggled and playfully batted me away. As this happened, I felt relieved. I saw in her eyes love that only sisters could share, and this made me feel better about burning my paws for her.

We crawled into the nearby tunnel, and I fell asleep that night knowing that Luna was safe.

THE LONG HUNT

The next morning, I awoke to a groaning sound. It seemed to be coming from Luna. "What's wrong?" I asked.

"My paw really hurts. It feels like it's on fire!" she answered. I rose to my paws and walked over to her. Her small left front paw was the color of one of the bright red berries that Mom used to tell us not to eat. Upon hearing the conversation, Tango woke up and trotted over to us.

"It looks like you burned your paw from that tree," said Tango. He went over to the back of the tunnel and scraped some soft, moist dirt up from the ground. Then, he came over to Luna and buried her paw in it.

"Hey, it feels cooler now," exclaimed Luna. "Thanks, Tango!"

"You're welcome," Tango replied.

Even though my siblings seemed to be doing fine, I felt like I couldn't breath. I was not used to being underground, so I crawled out of the damp tunnel and into the cool, fresh air.

I decided to go on a walk, so I tramped through the colorful leaves that led to the river. We had decided to call it the "Deathflow" since Tango almost died there because of how strongly the current was flowing. We also had a name for the burning tree. It was the "Blazewood Oak," and it was a bit of a longer walk to get there than the Deathflow, but it still wasn't the longest of ways.

As I neared the Deathflow, I tried to practice fishing. I remembered that when I was a kitten, I witnessed a raccoon fishing. It looked fairly simple, so I decided to try it out. I stuck my paw in the water when I saw a trout go by, but it did me no good. I realized that fishing wasn't that easy after all, and that I needed more practice. I was really hungry, and I wanted to feed my siblings, too. I sat down and waited for another fish to come by.

After a while, I gave up and decided to go hunt in the forest. This time, I caught a rabbit and a squirrel, and I felt really lucky that I had a good hunt. I brought back the food to my siblings in the tunnel. They wolfed it down, leaving only a bit for me.

"Hey!" I shouted, "I am the one who caught that food. I should be able to eat it!"

They bowed their heads in shame. "We're sorry," apologized Luna.

I looked at them for a minute, and then I tried my best to

dismiss it. I nibbled on what was left of the delicious prey as my stomach scolded me for not having enough to eat.

Later that night, I heard another groan from Luna. I also heard Tango burying Luna's paw again, and telling her that the burn wouldn't last forever, and that she would heal. I fell back asleep after that.

When I woke up the next morning, I felt famished. I slipped out of the tunnel and prowled around the forest. A cold breeze weaved its way in and out through my coat. It felt like all the animals had left the forest. Winter was almost here and prey was scarce. My stomach was the only thing that I cared about right now, so I made my way to the Deathflow to drink and try to calm my stomach. When I started to lap up the water, I felt an icy chill go through me. That water was freezing!

I was now ravenously hungry, so I decided the only thing I could do was to go fishing. Much to my disappointment, the difficulty still remained the same. It seemed like all the fish in this river had swum past, and I was too slow to catch them. Just when I was about to give up, a brown fish about as thick as a young oak branch swam into my view. I aimed my paw, steadied my balance, and waited. Suddenly, before I even knew what I was doing, instinct took over and I hurled my paw through the icy water. The fish took the worst of the blow, and it flew out of the river and landed right beside me. I was so stunned, I almost let it flop back into the water and swim away. Thankfully, I snapped out of my trance and sunk my teeth into its scaly skin. There was a snap. The fish lay limp in my jaws.

My catch and I, with the help of my swift movements, were soon back at the tunnel. I showed my catch to Luna and Tango and then started to scarf it down. This time, Tango and Luna got the small pieces, because they were not as hungry as me because of last night's dinner. This time, I went to sleep with a full stomach and the taste of the fish still lingering on my tongue.

A STRANGE ENCOUNTER

The next morning, I awoke to a nice feeling of satisfaction. I had caught a fish yesterday, and I wanted to catch another one today. I walked down to the Deathflow. I was about to lap up some of the water when I heard something.

"***Bam!***" My tail puffed up as big as a fallen log as I rushed back toward the tunnel.

"Luna, Tango, follow me! There is something going on outside!" I yowled.

They joined me by my side as we rushed down to where I had heard the noise. Then, we saw him. It was a weird monster thing with two legs too short and two legs too long. It stood up on its hind feet like a grizzly bear, yet it didn't have any fur. It had colorful skin, and it was holding something sharp while whacking a tree with it. It murmured while it attacked the oak, "It's gonna be a cold winter this year. I sure hope this tree comes down soon, or I might just freeze to death!" He chuckled to himself, and then continued whacking the tree.

I didn't know what that thing was, but the sharp metal thing was making big dents in that tree. I decided I didn't want to stick around anymore. "Guys, let's leave," I urged. "I don't want that monster to see us."

"Ok," replied Tango.

We started to walk back to the tunnel when Luna tripped over a stick and fell. There was a crunching sound as she landed on the dry leaves.

"Huh? Who's there?" the thing said as it looked around. Then, it started to walk toward us. I wanted to move, but my legs felt limp! I was frozen with fear as the thing walked over.... and saw us!

"Oh," it exclaimed, "what cute kittens! I'm gonna have to call the animal shelter again. If people would just keep their pets inside!" He walked over to a toolbox and picked it up. Then he came over to us. I tried to get away, but I felt too scared to move! He put his hands around us, and even though we tried kicking and meowing and scratching and squirming, he would not let go. We watched helplessly as he placed us in his toolbox. Then he picked up his sharp stick.

"Ok, calm down," I urged. "We just need to get out of this box. When I say 'meow,' we'll all do whatever it takes to get away from this thing." Tango and Luna nodded their heads in agreement.

"Meow!" I yowled at the top of my lungs.

"Whoa!" exclaimed the thing, and he dropped the toolbox in surprise.

After we clattered to the ground, my siblings and I succeeded in pushing the lid of the toolbox open. We all bolted away from the strange creature and, though he was determined, he was too slow as we darted around the forest. We slid into the tunnel and down the damp soil until each of us landed at the bottom.

"Is he gone?" I asked anxiously.

"I don't know, Autumn," replied Tango. "I'll go check the entrance." He crept slowly toward the opening in our tunnel and peeked out the other end. He swung his head left to right as his gaze darted back and forth like startled grasshoppers. "All clear," he meowed, and added under his breath softly, "I hope."

ON THE MOVE

The days after that, we had discussions in our tunnel more often than before. We were all trying to answer one question. Believe it or not, all of these meetings were just about that one question. We were just trying to decide whether it was safe for us to stay in the tunnel, or if we had to move on away from it to a place where we could have a better chance of finding Mom.

We finally decided that we were going to have to leave. None of us wanted to leave the earthy tunnel that had sheltered us for so many nights in a row, but we had to. We left the morning after the decision was made. We didn't really say much, so it was pretty quiet the whole way.

I missed Mom more and more every day now. I felt like I would never see her again. I also missed the tunnel. It provided good shelter, and I was starting to get used to sleeping on the damp soil. The walk was long. We didn't really have a destination; we just wanted to have a safe place to stay.

After walking for a while, my legs started to feel like limp mouse tails. I was tired and hungry. On top of all this, the winter frost had arrived. It came as a swirling wind, nipping at my nose and my ears.

"I can't walk any farther," I announced. "It's just too cold, and I'm too hungry to be walking around the woods without feeling tired!"

Luna paused and looked at me. "You're right," Luna agreed. "It is going to get really cold really fast, so we'd better stop walking. You two can go get comfortable in that dry ditch. It looks safe to me, since there seems to be an old willow that fell over it. I will do the hunting this time because you have been so helpful, Autumn. I'll meet you guys there!"

As she galloped off through the woods, Tango and I climbed down the steep dirt walls that led into the ditch. I landed with a thud in the trench. When I got up and shook the dust from my fur, I accidently sprayed Tango with soil from my pelt. He gave me a playful glare, and then pounced on me! I rolled over in the dirt with Tango still on top of me.

"Oh, it's on, you big puffball!" I shouted as I pushed myself up to my feet. Tango then lost his hold on my back, and he slid off me and into the dry dirt below. He hissed playfully. I got a running start and tackled him with all my strength. He fell back on the ground. Then, looking stunned, he got up and licked his paw awkwardly. I knew this meant that even though he wasn't hurt, he was surprised at my strength, and a bit embarrassed that he didn't win.

"I'm back with a rabbit!" I heard Luna shout as she jumped into the ditch next to us. Hanging from her mouth was a plump, limp rabbit. She dropped it next to us. "Dig in," she said cheerfully.

We all ate together that evening. Feeling the delicious meat slip down my throat brought back memories of Mom feeding us. Then, without warning, I started to yowl. The sound echoed among the mountains and trees. I yowled again, and this time Tango and Luna joined in. We all sat there, yowling in sadness for losing our mother.

It didn't last long, however, for we tired quickly, so we laid down next to each other. I stared up at the sky. The stars shined brightly. I tried to recall something that Mom had told us about stars but, before I could remember, my eyes fluttered closed, and I gave in to the pull of sleep.

NEW DAY, NEW FRIENDS

The next morning, I awoke to the shuffling of leaves. I lifted my head slowly so I wouldn't disturb my siblings sleeping next to me, and climbed out of the ditch. I looked around. Then, I saw a shadow. I let out a deep hiss. The shadow then walked toward me. I puffed up my fur and arched my back, so the animal would know I would fight. Then I saw her. She was an older golden tabby cat who reminded me of someone.

"Mom!" I shouted.

"What?" said the golden tabby. "I'm sorry, there must be some mistake, young kitten. I am not your mom. My name is Dawn."

Oh, I thought, as I tried to hide my embarrassment. I had assumed that because her coat was about the same color that she was Mom. I spoke with Dawn a bit more, and I found out she meant no harm at all, and only wanted to see how we were doing. Apparently, she had seen us arrive here.

Just then, Tango and Luna came to join me. It took me a while to introduce Dawn and say that she was not a threat. Then, after we all calmed down, I asked if Dawn wanted to travel with us.

"I would love to!" she exclaimed.

We started walking and, along the way, Dawn told us about how she was bored and lonely in the big forest and was hungry for some company and adventure. After more curious looks and plentiful questions, she continued. Her parents had disappeared during a hunting trip when she was younger. She then said that after this tragic event, she had to recall and use her parents' survival information to help herself get used to the sudden fresh start in life. For a few winters now, she had been on her own.

We all were silent for a moment to take this information in, and then my sister seized the opportunity to tell her our story. Luna explained about our lost mother while Tango caught us another rabbit. Since there were now four of us, the meal wasn't very big, but Dawn seemed eager to help us, and we wanted to make her feel like she was part of the group.

After we finished eating, we continued to walk. I was trotting along on the dirt floor of the woods when there was a rustle of leaves near us. I saw Dawn shake her head in the direction of the sound.

"What was that?" I asked.

"Nothing," Dawn quickly answered.

We kept walking for a long time. Finally, we stopped at a small stream to take a break. Tango was lapping up some puddle water when, all of a sudden, a furry body streaked past us and tackled Tango! There was a series of yowls and hisses before Dawn yelled something over to the other cat attacking my brother.

"Fern, stop!" she commanded the other cat. "I thought we agreed that you wouldn't attack them!"

The cat called "Fern" released his hold on my brother, and slowly walked up to Dawn. "I'm sorry, Dawn," he said apologetically. "I just wanted to protect you. I don't want you to get hurt." Then, he turned to face us. "I'm very sorry about that. I just find myself a little overprotective of my sister, that's all."

Tango nodded his head, signaling that he forgave Fern. Then he went over to the puddle to continue drinking.

I turned to look at Fern. He was purring and entwining tails with Dawn. I felt like I should go and look for clues for Mom right then, partly because I felt as if Fern would have to apologize to Tango, (and I wasn't in the mood to witness the awkwardness that would come along with it) and partly because I might find something, even though the chances would be slim because of the amount of time we had been apart. Everyone was either resting or drinking, so I decided I would go alone.

After my siblings and I agreed on this plan, I started to walk into another part of the woods. The birds chirped over my head, letting out angry cries as crows toyed with them. The squirrels scaled the trees easily as they jumped from limb to limb, trying to find more food for the winter that would soon be upon us. I laid down and scanned the ground for paw prints, but there were no signs of Mom to be found.

I heard Tango call for me to come. I answered with a high-pitched meow, and then I streaked through the woods and leaped, landing right beside Tango.

A few minutes later, we were back to hiking through the woods. The scene of the forest started to sooth me, until it suddenly hushed. Something was wrong. I looked around, but found to my surprise no one else seemed to have noticed the change. I tried to tell myself that nothing was wrong, and I started to calm down a tad, until I saw a figure emerge from a bush. A fox! She started creeping toward us. Then, she jumped. She jumped into the air, and came down right in front of Fern. He hissed in surprise and fear, and then he bolted. We followed Fern swiftly as the fox came near us, its jaws snapping in hunger.

"Over here into this small hole! The fox can't reach us there!" Dawn yelled. We didn't even think about questioning her. We dove down into the hole, with the fox digging and barking at the entrance.

"What do we do now?" Luna asked in a quiet, shaky voice.

"We wait," answered Fern, who was still recovering from the surprise of a fox appearing in front of him.

Soft dirt tumbled down from the entrance as we waited. The fox seemed to be getting tired of batting pointlessly at the entrance of the small hole and, after what seemed like forever, she got up and slowly paced away.

We emerged from the hole cautiously. After making sure

the fox was gone, we started to walk again. It was getting dark, and the darker it got the more frightened I became. If the fox was out there, who knows what other predators could be lurking behind the trees?

I started to grow drowsy, and pretty soon I was on the verge of collapsing right on the spot and going out like a firefly in the morning. Dawn seemed to notice how I was struggling to keep my eyes open because she stopped and said, "How about we take shelter here for the night? I think we all need a bit of rest after a very long day."

We all agreed. I can't remember much about what happened after that. I only remember lying down to watch Dawn and the others make a den. I must have dosed off right about then because the rest is foggy.

WINTER BEGINS

The next morning, I opened my eyes to the sound of stamping feet. When I got up, I saw it was a small group of rabbits. I realized I could impress everyone if I caught two full-sized rabbits. I started off towards them. I chose my position carefully. I knew if I wanted this prey to be mine that I had to be silent and swift. Before I knew it, I was in a good range to strike. I positioned myself, got ready, and then saw something black swoop down and squawk at them, and all the rabbits started hopping away! I recognized its hoarse cries at once. It was a crow!

I was so frustrated I sprinted out where the rabbits were. I scanned the treetops with my eyes until I finally spotted it. Then it started to turn its head in my direction. For one eerie moment, the crow and I locked eyes. I felt a mixture of anger and confusion. This crow had just made me lose some important food, and why was it by itself? I was about to pounce at it when Tango came crashing through the vegetation and nearly ran me over. Startled, the crow quickly flew away.

"Where were you?" he asked in a worried tone.

"I just wanted to catch some food. I would have been back at our den by now with lots of delicious prey if it hadn't been for that crow!" I complained.

"Well, the others are worried, so let's get back to the den, ok?" Tango started walking back.

I followed him. At the den, I was surprised to find everyone eating. "How did you guys get that food?" I asked.

"It turns out that Dawn and Fern are really great squirrel hunters!" Luna said with her mouth still full of food.

I felt a bit annoyed when I heard this, but I tried my best to dismiss it. There would always be more rabbits in the future. After I calmed down, I started to dig in. Squirrels in the winter were always plump and delicious because of the squirrels digging up and eating their nuts. This meant that the squirrels you did catch were always very pleasant to eat. The rich meat filled my mouth and my mood changed to a pleasant one as I munched on the prey.

When everyone was finished eating, we decided to set off again. We started walking towards a field in the distance. I was starting to get discouraged about Mom and how we might never find her again. The forest was so big and vast that the chances of finding her were not exceptionally high. However, I kept walking into the bushes and around damp logs and over crunchy leaves.

Then I felt it: the cold breeze. It wove its way through the fur on my back and in and out of tree branches. I looked around, searching for something I wasn't sure I knew about. I looked up and saw little white dots drifting down from the sky. "What is happening?" I asked.

"It's snow," replied Dawn. "It falls every winter here in the forest. I think it is made out of little icicles."

The stuff kept falling, and pretty soon my fur was coated in it. We all kept walking towards the field, but it soon became obvious that it was getting too cold to proceed. The snow seemed everywhere now. I felt too tired to keep going. I looked up, but all I saw was white. The frost stung my fur like a million bees, and I couldn't keep going. I looked around once more, but that only confirmed it. I was lost and alone in the cold night. Cold and hungry, I found a big oak tree with wide branches and leaves. I settled down under it into a spot in the roots. The snow was not as bad here, yet it still blinded me from everything even a meter away. I closed my eyes and fell asleep.

I awoke to find it snowing a lot lighter than before. I decided to keep walking and try to find the others. I was very discouraged because of the fact that I had lost not just Mom, but Tango, Luna, Fern, and Dawn, too. I was about to plop into the snow when I heard voices.

SQUIRREL FIASCO

"...but we have to keep looking!"

"No, we must stay here in case Autumn comes back!"

"Did you guys see the... It kept flying over here. I don't know why."

I meowed to them. In return, I heard their voices high and happy, as they seemed to fly over the snow in graceful leaps.

"Autumn! We've found you!" mewed Luna. I started to purr contentedly, and then Luna joined in too. We all started purring, until we sounded like a hoard of happy cicadas.

After the happy mood started to die down, I showed them

the tree that I was at, and we agreed to stay there as long as was needed. We all made ourselves at home at it, and I was able to regain my energy. After resting and chatting among one another for a little bit, Luna spoke up.

"I," Luna paused as her stomach growled loudly, "need to find some food!"

"I will go," announced Dawn.

"No, I will," I declared. "We all need to do our part, and last time we ate it was your catch. Now it's my turn to go."

Dawn nodded and nuzzled me. "Be careful out in the snow," she warned. "We don't want you getting lost again."

Fern smiled at that remark. I said goodbye and then started off. I was feeling confident I would catch something good today. Plus, that crow wouldn't follow us this far…. would it? I tried to take my mind off of it by playing a game. I counted all the paw prints I made in the soft snow as I walked along. Then I heard something. It was a rustling noise. There was prey somewhere!

I crept along slowly, making sure I didn't make a sound. Even though the snow was lighter, I still could not see that well. I realized I was going to have to rely more on my ears then my eyes for this hunt. I could soon make out a blurry shape at the base of a tree. It was a squirrel! A large one, too. Slowly, I got closer, and closer, and…I pounced! I guess the snow made my aim a bit off though, as I landed face first into the snow. I had felt the squirrel's silky pelt brush against me as I pounced. I got up and spun around. My world had become this squirrel.

I watched as, in panic, it started to scale the nearest pine tree. I quickly started to climb in pursuit. However, I didn't think about what I was doing. Higher and faster we climbed, until the squirrel turned onto a branch next to him. I followed. The branch swayed as we both raced across it. Thankfully, the branch was thick enough to support our weight, or I might have fallen to my doom.

The squirrel, while running, looked back to see if I was still following. It didn't take long for it to pay for its mistake. It slipped off the branch, but caught itself just as it was about to fall onto the cold ground below. However, even though the squirrel caught itself, it didn't have time to get back onto the branch. I carefully but swiftly ran to the squirrel and caught it between my teeth. I took a minute to regain my strength, and as I sat there and tasted the delicious meat I slowly returned to my senses. I was very high up, and I had no idea how to get down.

I started to get angry with myself for being hunger driven and getting into this mess. The branch suddenly started to crack in the freezing cold weather, a sound that reminded me of noises that the monster's sharp stick made, and panic rose in me. The branch was going to fall! I looked down and decided that I had to jump to the trunk of the tree. I started counting.

"1!" I focused on the tree trunk.

"2!" I gripped the prey tighter in my mouth.

"3!" I leaped up into the air. I was almost there!

I was about to grip the trunk when I looked down. So far down…I looked at the branch I was on. It seemed like it was getting farther away. I was falling! I scrambled madly in the air. I needed to get a landing point. Something slammed into my side. It was a branch, and I reacted fast and grabbed the next branch after it. I stayed there for a few moments to try to catch my breath, and then I pushed my claws firmly into the frosty bark to pull myself up. I finally managed to get up onto the branch.

With the squirrel still clutched in my mouth, I looked around. I was too cold and afraid to go anywhere, and my body ached from slamming into that branch. I started to yowl loudly in hopes that someone would hear me. Night started to fall, and I was worried I would be stuck there.

Then, I heard noises. It sounded like crunching. I sprung up and looked around. The squirrel started to slip from my mouth, but I caught it just in time. I tasted blood; squirrel blood. It was then that I realized I had been gnawing on the squirrel. I scolded myself at the same time I heard someone.

"Autumn! Where are you? Are you all right?"

I wasted no time in answering. "I'm up here," I shouted, "in this tree!" I looked around and saw the amber eyes of Luna coming toward me.

"Why are you in a tree?" she questioned, looking confused.

"It's a long story. I'll tell you about it when we get home."

She still looked perplexed, but she just came over to the tree. "Jump down! You're not very high up, so you can land on me."

I gave her a worried look, but she just shook her head and spread her paws out to brace herself. I loosened my grip on the tree, closed my eyes, and leapt. I was suspended in air for a few seconds, and then I landed on a furry body.

"Oof!" she wheezed. I jumped off of her and she got up. "Let's get going back to the oak tree you found earlier. The others are waiting there for you."

We started to walk along the snowy earth. The stars shown brightly above us, and I thought for a second I saw three figures move among the stars. When I looked again, however, they were gone.

Later, we reached the oak tree. No one noticed me come back to the tree; they were all busy sleeping in a big pile to conserve heat. I curled up into a big ball of fluff and buried my nose into my paws. I started thinking about the cats I was traveling with. So far, they'd proven to be loyal and friendly. I started to purr softly. Even though the night was cold with frost, I felt warm and content. I was lulled to sleep that night by the crickets and the soft song of the wind.

FISHING AND DANCING

The next morning, I was the first one to open my eyes. I wondered if I should go hunting again, but then I saw the mangled squirrel and thought better of it. Even though I was hungry, I didn't want to wake the others up (and I was a bit embarrassed of my catch), so I started hopping from root to root around the tree trunk. However, at times I can be a bit clumsy. I was about to clear the longest jump for the 4th time when I tripped and fell on top of Tango.

"Ouch!" he exclaimed.

"Um, sorry Tango. I didn't mean to fall on you. I was just trying out my new game."

He sighed and got up. Drowsily, he walked over to the ripped squirrel and cocked his head. "What did you do to this? It looks like it got dropped from the top of the

Blazewood Oak."

I swiped my paw around nervously in the cold soil. "Um, its kind of a long story. I'll tell it to you later."

He nodded slowly and then returned to the shelter of the oak roots to wake the others. Soon, everyone was up and ready for breakfast. When they saw what actually was breakfast, I received a lot of questioning looks. Guilt pored through me like a river, and I prodded the dirt so many times in my nervousness that I soon succeeded in making a small hole.

"Um, well…" I trailed off in mid-sentence.

To my huge relief, Dawn stood up and said, "Ok, everyone, let's eat."

The others seemed to hear the hint of commanding in the sentence because they all quickly started to eat the torn squirrel. I still felt guilty about the prey I had caught, but that only added to my determination to catch something good. Suddenly, I had an idea to make up for what I had caught.

"Does anyone know about a river nearby?" I asked.

Fern's face lit up. "I do! I was here before when I wanted to go exploring once. There's one not far from here. I can show you it if you want me to."

I poked my tail into the air. "That would be awesome, Fern."

We started to hike to our destination. Soon, we were staring at a small river with various fish inside.

"I have an idea for a game," I declared. "We will have a contest to see who can catch the most fish from now until the furry ball is straight up in the sky. It will not only be fun and challenging, but also we will get prey to eat."

"Ok!" chorused everyone.

We all started waiting and watching. At one point, Tango and Fern were so intent on catching a fish that when they both saw the same perch, they swiped their paws so fast that, somehow, they both ended up falling in! At this sight, I fell back laughing so hard that I misdirected the fish I was holding in my mouth and, instead of putting it in my fish pile, I swung it around, missed my shot, and ended up hitting Luna in the face with the fish. Dawn thought this was positively hilarious, and she started to purr loudly from a mix of laughter and amusement. By the time everyone calmed down, the competition was over. Together, we had caught eight fish. Everyone was very pleased with him or herself. We started comparing the fish we had caught. It turned out that I was the winner!

I felt like I could dance, so I did. I scratched my claws on an old rotting log next to me, and everyone fell silent and looked at me. Then, I started to dance. I swung my tail around my head and pranced around in the frosty grass. I felt rejoiced that I could finally do something right! I twitched my ears and rolled in the leaves. Everyone was watching me in awe. They had never seen me dance before.

Then Dawn called "DANCE PARTY!" and they all joined in. Of course, some dance moves were better than others, but we all were just prancing around because we felt like doing it. The rest of the day seemed to fly by. My friends kept making up new games, and we were so busy goofing off and playing that it seemed like someone threw time out the window. One minute we were dancing, the next minute it was dark outside.

"Guys, I think we should start heading back to the oak," said Fern. "It's getting late and, I don't know about you, but I would not enjoy being eaten by wolves."

We all were instantly reminded of the night predators, and we began our journey back to the roots of the oak tree. As we reached the tree, we heard panting and crunching leaves.

"Umm, guys?" asked Luna. "I think something is following us…"

I turned around. There were shadows in the bushes by us.

"Get up the tree now!" shouted Tango. I shot up that tree like a cheetah on roller skates, which would have been fine if I didn't ram my head into a branch while doing so. This startled me and messed up my next move of climbing, so I started falling fast, and then suddenly I was suspended in air. Dawn had grabbed me by the scruff of my neck.

"Dawn, can I come up now?" I quickly asked, my paws shaking slightly from the terrifying event.

She seemed so triumphant in catching me that she had forgotten I was dangling off the edge of a branch with wolves jumping at me. "Oh," she smiled shyly. "Sorry, Autumn." She hauled me back onto the oak branch, where I sat panting hard for the next couple of minutes.

"Are we all ok?" asked Fern.

Everyone nodded, for most of us were too out of breath to speak.

"So, I guess we sleep here tonight," I suggested.

"Ok," said Tango.

We were still awake for a while after that. The branches of the tree were hard and scratchy with bark, and once anyone did close their eyes, it was hard not to think about the hungry carnivores down below us. However, somehow I eventually managed to go to sleep.

DOVES AND DRAMA

That night, I dreamed about dancing fish and wolves falling in streams. I ended up laughing myself awake. Tango was staring at me in curiosity.

"Ummm…" I had nothing to say.

"What's so hilarious?" Tango asked me impatiently.

"Nothing, just a weird dream. The others aren't up yet, and the wolves are gone. Want to go for a morning hunt?"

"Are you kidding me?" Tango whisper-shouted. "Of course! Let's go!"

We climbed down the tree (I did anyway; Tango half climbed and half fell down) and then started walking towards an open patch of land. There were a few doves

41

there on the ground. We couldn't speak to each other, or we might've frightened them away. Instead, we communicated by signals and instincts. One crouch, two tail flicks, stalk and sit again. We were in sync, and we were also very close to the doves. I nodded to Tango, who nodded back.

I crouched low in the grass, and then flew up into the air like an unleashed slinky. The doves made frantic movements to get away, but we were not going to give up easily. We ran like the wind underneath them. I knew that I could only catch them by jumping. I sprung into the air, and hit Tango! Maybe we were a little too in sync. We crashed into each other, and then fell back to the ground.

"NO!" yelled Tango. "We almost had one!"

"I know, bu-" Something was moving from under me. I slowly got to my paws, and a dove flew out! Unfortunately for the dove, it had taken a bad fall and was not prepared to take flight again. I launched myself at the dove, caught it, and then rolled onto the grass. I was about to shout "Hooray" when I realized I had rolled too far and I was now beginning to careen down a steep hill.

"Autumn, come back!" Tango yelled, as if I could.

He jumped down onto the hill and started chasing after me. The hill ended up being too steep for him, though, and he tumbled head over tail down it. Still clutching the dove in my paws, I shut my eyes. Suddenly, everything went black.

Three cats surrounded me. The first one had a silky white pelt. The second one had a ruffled grey coat. The third had deep blue fur. They paced around me and lifted me off the hill, and settled me onto a grassy patch. And then wolves took their places. The wolves bit me with their sharp teeth, again and again, and they kept chanting my name. "Autumn, Autumn!"

"What?" I opened my eyes. My friends were standing over me.

Tango spoke, "Autumn, you fell down the hill and blacked out. The others came as well, for they heard the commotion. Are you alright?"

"Umm, yeah, I guess so." When Tango gave me a suspicious look, I added, "I'm fine, really. Now let's go back to the tree. I'm hungry for some fish."

They all exchanged glances as I walked away from them. After a bit, they started to follow. I was storming off to the tree when I realized I had nothing to be mad about, and that they were just concerned about me. I felt a little better then, and I stopped walking so briskly and relaxed a little. When I did relax, something dropped onto the ground, and I realized why they had been looking at me weirdly. I'd still had the dove in my mouth. I purred a little in amusement. I needed to start keeping track of my food!

When I got back to the tree, I settled down by the roots and started to think about Mom. We hadn't gone anywhere for the past couple of days, and I was worried we would never find her if we didn't start moving.

"Can everyone come here please?" I asked. They started to gather around the tree with questioning looks on their faces. "This is our third day being here at this tree. If we want to find Mom, then we have to start looking. I say tomorrow we leave here, and start searching. Does anyone have any place in mind to go?"

They all looked at each other and, after they were done letting what I had said sink in, Luna spoke up. "We could go to that tall cliff over there," she paused to point her paw to the towering figure in the distance, "I'm sure if Mom wanted to find us, and we all know she does, then she would go somewhere easy to see. Maybe she thought that a big cliff would catch our attention."

I nodded in agreement. "Good idea, Luna. I think we should leave tomorrow. Besides, we aren't making any progress by sitting around this tree. It's starting to get dark, so let's eat and go to bed."

It looked like they agreed with what I had announced. After a brief conversation about the cliff and timing, I started to nudge the dove over to the food pile, and we all started to dig in. While I was eating, I found a plump rabbit in the food pile as well. When I finished questioning the others, I knew that Fern had gone hunting while we were gone.

After our filling meal, I trotted over to a small spot by our tree and sat down. I sat there for a while, and soon my siblings came and joined me. We didn't say much, but I was almost certain we were all thinking about Mom.

I watched the colors spread across the sky like a beautiful field of flowers, all mixed into one another, and all in full bloom. I felt a frosty breeze tickle my whiskers, and I scooted closer to my siblings. After gazing at the sky again, I noticed the fuzzy yellow ball descending from its perch in the colorful sky. I felt as if it was important, and that it wasn't yellow, but golden. After pondering this for a few minutes, I gave up on the hypothesis and wiggled even closer to my siblings.

After the light started to fade into the darkness of dusk,

Tango stood up and motioned back to the tree. Luna and I followed him as we all trotted back to the oak where our friends were. After bidding each other goodnight, I snuggled into one of the oak's smooth roots and drifted into a dreamless sleep.

THE CLIFF

I woke to a paw poking me in my ear. "Hey, what gives?" I asked in annoyance.

"Its time to proceed to the tall cliff, remember?" said Luna.

I got up and yawned. "Ok, let's go."

We started to walk, and after a long while we decided to take a break and let our energy refill. Once we regained our strength, we continued. We traveled until night, which was when we reached the cliff.

"I think I see a cave," declared Fern. "Let's rest there tonight."

We climbed up the cliff, which was thankfully not that steep. Fern motioned for us to follow him, so we did. We ended up standing by the mouth of the cave.

"Let's go in," Dawn whispered.

I carefully followed the others into the cave; there was something not right in there. As I snuck into a space that I wanted to sleep in, I tripped and fell onto something furry. A growl echoed through the dark cavern. I recognized the sound at once.

"Wolves, run!" I shouted.

We all bolted out of the cave and down the hill. As if one wolf wasn't enough, the whole pack had been awoken by the thunderous growl.

"Turn this way!" commanded Fern. We all made a sharp turn left, but I was so paranoid of falling off the cliff that I slowed as I ran around the corner. It was a big mistake to do so. The wolves were terrifyingly close to me, and I could almost feel their breath on my fur. Suddenly, a paw hit me, and I lost my balance and toppled over.

My eyes closed, and then I saw them: three star cats. A storm of memories flew around me. The Golden Fur; the star cats, Cloud, Wind and Rain; the wolves that almost caught the spirits of the sky; and, most importantly, Mom and her stories. I saw the star cats nod at me, and then they meowed at the sky. It was a sonorous sound, and it filled the air and flew on the wind.

Then my eyes flew open due to a loud "*Caw!*" and I saw a familiar crow. He was flying in the faces of the wolves, causing them to lose focus on me. I sat up but, before I started to run, I thought I saw him wink at me. I tore down the cliff to catch up with the others.

"Hello?" I called. There was a meow. "Finally, I found you guys. You left me there!" I said angrily as I walked toward the figure. I noticed that she looked older than the others.

"Autumn?" she said.

"Mom?" I questioned.

"Autumn, where have you been? I thought I had lost you!" she exclaimed.

We purred and entwined tails. It seemed as if nothing could go wrong at this moment. My emotions seemed so strong and jubilant that it felt as if they could lift the sky. And, to make things even better, I heard voices coming from a different path down the cliff.

"Autumn! Mom!" Tango and Luna shouted. They ran up to Mom and jumped on her. We were all so happy we were finally reunited.

"Who are they?" Mom said after we were done laughing, for she had noticed Fern and Dawn. They came over to her. "I'm Fern, and that's my sister, Dawn. We accompanied your kittens on the journey here to find you, but since that's been done, I guess we'll go. It was nice meeting you, Mrs...." he trailed off.

"Summer," Mom finished for him, "and you don't have to go. I wouldn't mind at all if you stayed with us."

My tail pointed to the sky in excitement. Dawn looked at Fern, and they started to whisper in low voices to each other.

"I think," said Dawn, "that staying is a great idea!" she

finished happily.

"Yes!" my siblings and I chorused.

"I'm glad you would like to. Now let's go rest. Our new home is not too far away from here," Mom said. "This is a place we will not have to leave any time soon, for there are animals and rivers for us to get supplies. Follow me." We did as we were told, and soon we came to a large, sturdy pine tree.

"Cool," said Tango casually. "It looks a bit plain, though."

"Look on the other side of it," Mom answered.

I went around the massive tree and, there in the middle of the trunk, was a hole. I jumped inside. It was wonderful! The smell of pine needles lingered, and there were soft, colorful leaves on the floor.

"I love it!" I told Mom.

"I'm glad," she replied. "Now let's get some rest."

We all curled up in the den and, before we went to sleep, Mom told the story of The Golden Fur to us and Dawn and Fern, and all the memories came rushing back. When she finished, I rested my head on my paws and knew that deep down inside me some urge had been satisfied. As the Golden Fur set in the forest that I had traveled in for so many days, I knew that I would always stay close to my family.

ABOUT THE AUTHOR

Lillian Hughes was a 10-year-old girl when she started to write this. Having a passion for writing, she started to make a story on her computer about a group of kids who had a ghost problem. However, the idea fizzled out after three pages, when she decided that the plot would be too short and hard to follow.

Fortunately, this did not take away her dream of writing a book, so she decided to write about something she was passionate about: cats. She had two cats, one named Julius, and his sister, Panchey. Unfortunately, she forgot about the book, and then for a while didn't feel like working on it. Then, Panchey passed away. Lillian was depressed, and suddenly she felt like working on her story. She continued it for Panchey, and all the other cats out there.

When she finished writing it (at age 11), she felt very excited and, with the help of her mom's editing, and her dad's graphic designs, The Golden Fur was complete. To this day, she still does not know where she got the idea of three cats going on an adventure, to chase the sun and be guided by spirit cats. She does now know, however, that if you are ever lost or in trouble, just follow the Golden Fur. ☺

Made in the USA
Columbia, SC
23 April 2018